Holiday Hassle!

Millie and Bombassa

Be sure to read:

Cash Crazy!

Dizzy D.I.Y.!

... and lots, lots more!

Holiday Hassle!

written and illustrated by
Shoo Rayner

■SCHOLASTIC

Scholastic Children's Books,
Commonwealth House, 1-19 New Oxford Street,
London, WC1A 1NU, UK
a division of Scholastic Ltd
London ~ New York ~ Toronto ~ Sydney ~ Auckland
Mexico City ~ New Delhi ~ Hong Kong

First published by Scholastic Ltd, 2003

ISBN 0 439 98133 6

Printed and bound by Oriental Press, Dubai, UAE

10 9 8 7 6 5 4 3 2 1

Chapter One

Bombassa opened one eye and peered out from under the duvet.

"Much too cold today," he groaned. He rolled over, snuggled down and went back to sleep.

He dreamed his favourite dream in which he owned a cafe, where he drank tea and ate biscuits all day.

After a while, a small, twittering voice broke into his dream and woke him up.

It was Millie, Bombassa's best friend. "Wakey, wakey! Rise and shine! Time to get going!"

Bombassa did not like being woken in the middle of his favourite dream.

"Time to get going for what?" he snapped.

"Well … um … er…" Millie struggled to find an answer. "Well, if you don't get going, you'll never know," she said, thinking quickly.

"Today will be just like yesterday, only colder," Bombassa complained. "My life is so boring. Nothing exciting ever happens. Every day is the same."

Millie sighed. It was going to be one of those days. "Oh dear! You are feeling sorry for yourself today. I think you need a holiday. After all, a change is as good as a rest."

"I'd rather just have the rest," said Bombassa, pulling the duvet back over his head.

Millie tapped her toes and shrugged her shoulders. "I suppose I'll just have to organize things myself."

ZZZZZZZ

Chapter Two

A little while later, Bombassa made himself a huge cup of tea.

As he sat up in bed, dunking biscuits in his tea, Millie returned with a pile of holiday brochures.

"Look at this!" Millie said, opening the first brochure. "Activity holidays! There's mountain climbing or canoeing or hang-gliding or … wow, bungee jumping!"

Bombassa didn't have to say a word.

His look said it all.

"Oh. Umm … maybe not," said Millie, tossing the brochure into the bin. "I don't suppose activity holidays are quite your sort of thing, are they?"

Bombassa still said nothing. He dunked a biscuit, dripped tea and crumbs all over the duvet and stared out of the window. He watched an aeroplane drift slowly across the sky.

"What about Spain?"
trilled Millie.
She flitted on to the
bedpost and began
flamenco dancing.

"*Viva España!* Golden beaches, endless
sunshine, the beautiful blue Mediterranean
Sea. What a place for a holiday!"

"Hmmf!" Bombassa grumbled. "I can't
speak Spanish, sand makes me itch, I'll get
sunburned and seasick and worst of all we'd
have to fly there.
I hate flying!"

"What!" Millie shot up into the air. "You hate flying? What is there to hate?"

She flew around the room, twisting and turning, flipping and flapping, swishing and swooshing.

"Wheeee!" she screamed as she dived between Bombassa's ears. "Flying is the best fun in the world."

Bombassa folded his arms and waited for
Millie to come back down to earth.
"I don't have wings!
I would have to
fly in a plane.
I don't like
flying in
planes."

"Have you ever been in a plane?" asked
Millie.

"Well, no … not exactly," Bombassa
replied. "But I'm sure I wouldn't like it."

Millie sorted through the rest of the brochures. "Okay, let's see what else there is."

Bombassa didn't like any of Millie's suggestions.

The last brochure was called *Tasteful Holidays*.

"This looks like a good brochure. It's for people who like their food!" Millie explained. "You could go to America and eat lobsters."

Bombassa stuck his tongue out, "Yuck!"

"Well, how about gherkins and pickles in Poland?"

"Eeeugh!" Bombassa moaned and clutched his tummy. "I hate pickles!"

Millie turned the page and smiled. "Oh, this is the holiday for you … no doubt about it."

"Oh yeah, sure," sighed Bombassa.

"No, honestly," said Millie excitedly.

Bombassa tried peeking over the top of the brochure, but he couldn't read it upside down. "Well, go on then … tell me."

Millie sighed. "No, you'd have to fly there, and you don't like flying."

Bombassa grabbed the brochure from Millie. As he read, a big smile crept over his face.

Tea for Two

This is the holiday for real tea drinkers!

"Yes! That's what I call a real holiday!" whooped Bombassa. In a trice he was under the bed, looking for his suitcase.

"But we'll have to go on a plane. You said you hated flying," said Millie, looking worried.

Bombassa smiled. "I'll be brave. I love tea much more than I hate flying."

Chapter Three

Packing was hard work. Bombassa wanted to take everything with him.

"You can't take your duvet!" Millie complained. "It's hot in India. You won't need a duvet."

"But I do like to be comfortable," Bombassa explained.

He wanted to take his kettle, teapot and mug. Millie sighed and shook her head.

"All right," said Bombassa, "but I'm taking my tea and biscuits."

"But there'll be plenty of tea in India," said Millie.

He wanted to take thirty-seven books.

Millie threw her wings up in the air. "But you only ever read two books in a whole year!"

And he wanted clothes for every season and type of weather.

"Just pack for warm weather," Millie pleaded.

After a lot of arguing she managed to cut down Bombassa's luggage from five large suitcases to only one.

"It's a good job you didn't pack *everything*," Millie said. "We're not going for another two weeks!"

Bombassa was so excited.
He could hardly wait
for the great
adventure to start.
Every morning
he woke up
and crossed
another day
off the calendar.

Every day it got colder. When the great
day arrived, it was snowing.

"N-n-n-never mind," shivered Millie as they waited for the taxi to take them to the airport. "It'll be n-n-nice and warm in India."

As soon as the taxi arrived, they put their cases in the boot and climbed inside.

But Bombassa couldn't settle in his seat. He kept remembering things that he'd forgotten.

"Oh my goodness!" he yelped. "I should turn the water off in case the pipes freeze." Then, "Did I lock the front door? I'd better go and check."

Millie was exasperated. "You've checked it three times already!" she twittered. "We're going to be late."

She needn't have worried.

Chapter Four

By the time they reached the airport, the snow had covered everything, turning it white.

They hurried to the check-in desk with minutes to spare.

Millie appealed to the mongoose behind the counter. "I hope we're not too late?"

The mongoose smiled. "I'm afraid the plane has been delayed because the runway is covered in snow."

Millie and Bombassa found a cafe, where they had tea and biscuits while they waited to hear about their flight.

They waited…

…and waited…

…and waited.

Once in a while, a voice came over the loudspeakers with an update.

"We're sorry no planes are flying at the moment. The snow is still falling so it is impossible to clear the runway."

Bombassa was soon bored. He twiddled his thumbs and drummed his fingers for a while.

He read a few magazines.

He looked out of the huge windows and
watched everything disappear under the
snow.

He played Rhino v Dino™ on a video machine but he wasn't very good!

"This is stupid! My rhino keeps falling into dino traps!" he moaned, as he lost another game.

He drank more tea. He dunked more biscuits.

No one was going anywhere. The airport was full of travellers who were going nowhere until the snow stopped.

At midnight everyone on Bombassa's flight was taken to the airport hotel for the night.

"Ah! Luxury," Bombassa sighed, as he snuggled into his bed and drifted off into his favourite dream again.

Chapter Five

In the morning, the snow had stopped, the
runway had been cleared and the airport
was working again.

Millie was relieved. "Thank heavens! I
really don't want to spend my holiday in
the airport hotel."

Bombassa didn't reply.
He was feeling very
nervous. He kept
twitching and
fiddling with
things.

"Are you going to be all right on the
plane?" Millie asked.

"Of course!" Bombassa growled back.

But he wasn't all right. When their flight
number was called, Bombassa felt sick.

They showed their passports and walked
to the corridor-like bridge that connected
to the door of the plane.

As they got nearer the door, Bombassa
walked more and more slowly. His stomach
felt as if a football team was practising
penalty shoot-outs inside! His head felt light
and dizzy.

When they got
to the door,
the stewardess
smiled sweetly.
"Welcome
aboard,"
she said.

As Bombassa turned to run he felt the
ground give way beneath his feet.

When he woke up, a sea of faces was staring down at him. Millie was furiously fanning his face with her wings.

"What's the matter? Bombassa, are you all right?"

It took him a moment to remember where he was. Then the panic started again.

"I can't do it, Millie. I can't get on the plane. I-I-I'm terrified of flying."

Bombassa's whole body was shaking.
A big tear rolled down his cheek.

"I thought I could do it. I really want
to go to India and drink all that tea, but
I can't get on the plane!"

"I'm afraid some animals are like that,"
said the stewardess. "Sadly, we can't let
you on the plane if you're really that scared
of flying."

Chapter Six

Millie and Bombassa stood outside the airport building and wondered what to do. Their suitcases were on the plane to India and wouldn't come back for three days.

"I know," said Bombassa. "I saw a sign at the hotel … let's go back there."

At the hotel desk, Bombassa pointed at a sign that read *Bed and Breakfast*.

"That's all I really want from a holiday," said Bombassa.

"That's all you ever want!" sighed Millie.

BED AND BREAKFAST

"Does bed and breakfast mean that I can have my breakfast in bed?" he asked the receptionist.

The receptionist nodded.

"And how many times a day can I have breakfast?" Bombassa asked, hopefully.

"As many times as you like," said the receptionist. "Just pick up the phone, dial 0 and call for room service."

Soon, Bombassa was in his hotel room, tucked up in bed, snug as a bug.

"This is not exactly a proper holiday," said Millie. "You spend most of your life in bed. This will be just like any other day in the year."

Bombassa beamed. "Yes! But don't you remember what you said? A change is as good as a rest. And this is a change."

Bombassa winked at Millie and leaned across the bed. He picked up the phone and dialled 0.

"Hello!" he boomed into the mouthpiece. "Is that room service? I'd like breakfast in bed, please ... with a large pot of tea ... a large pot of Indian tea!"